Willow
and the
Wedding

by: Denise Brennan-Nelson

Illustrated by: Cyd Moore

Willow hadn't slept much the night before. Uncle Ash was picking her up bright and early. They had a big day planned!

Their first stop was the animal shelter. They delivered the toys and treats they had collected. They cleaned pens, gave baths, and played with the animals.

They walked to the park and Uncle Ash pushed Willow on the merry-go-round. They fed the ducks and raced down the slides.

Afterward, they went to Squilly's for their favorite dessert—donuts!

Uncle Ash and Willow had a lot in common. They loved animals, adventure, and art. They had the same curly hair, blue eyes, and one dimple each. They even shared the same middle name.

But there was one thing they didn't share . . .

Willow loved to dance!

But when she tried to get Uncle Ash to join her, he was as stiff as Grandpa's cane.

"What's wrong?" Willow would ask.

"I don't dance," was all he would say.

Willow tried everything, but Uncle Ash wouldn't even tap his foot.

"Why doesn't Uncle Ash dance?" Willow asked Mama one day.

"He used to," Mama said wistfully. "Uncle Ash loved to dance, just like you do. And he was amazing!"

"What happened?" Willow asked.

"Well," Mama remembered, "it was a long time ago. Uncle Ash got the lead role in the school musical. He was so excited and he practiced every chance he had."

"On opening night he danced his heart out," Mama said. "But it didn't go the way he wanted it to."

"What do you mean?" Willow asked.

"The kids laughed at him. They called him 'Freakenstein' and 'Twinkle Toes.' And to make matters worse," Mama added, "Grandpa wasn't there. He didn't think much of Uncle Ash dancing."

Willow thought about Uncle Ash and how he must have felt when the kids laughed at him. She thought about Grandpa not being there and not wanting Uncle Ash to dance.

Mostly, though, Willow thought about what Mama had said: *Uncle Ash loved to dance.*

Uncle Ash and David came to dinner on Sunday. They had a special announcement to make. They were getting married! They asked Willow to be their flower girl. She pirouetted around the table.

"Yes! Yes! Yes!"

They talked about colors and candles and flowers.

They showed Willow and Mama photos of the beach where they were getting married.

And they talked about what they would serve for dinner and dessert.

"Donuts with sprinkles?" Willow said, hopeful.

"There's only one thing left," Mama said. "Music!"

"And dancing!" Willow exclaimed as she grabbed Uncle Ash's hands and pulled him up to dance.

But Uncle Ash didn't move.

"I'm afraid that's not going to happen," Uncle Ash said firmly. "Everyone knows I don't dance."

"Who will I dance with?" David asked.

"Willow," Uncle Ash replied. "Willow loves to dance."

A week later Willow, Mama, and Uncle Ash went shopping for a flower girl dress.

They picked out the most beautiful dress Willow had ever seen!

After lunch—and dessert at Squilly's—it was time for Willow's weekly dance class.

Uncle Ash turned to leave, but Willow had a plan.

"Come with us, Uncle Ash. You can watch me dance."

As the students stretched and chatted, Willow announced that her uncle was getting married.

And then, to Uncle Ash's surprise, Willow told the class how he loved to dance when he was young.

The music began to play. Uncle Ash watched Willow and the other children dancing and twirling and laughing.

Without realizing it, he began to tap his foot. And before he could stop her, Willow pulled Uncle Ash to his feet.

He felt awkward at first. He hadn't danced in years!

Miss Sally led the children through the moves and Uncle Ash followed along.

They practiced leaps . . . and twirls . . . and pliés.

When the tempo picked up they did the shuffle and the stomp.

They did toe rises and jazz walks and attitude turns.

Miss Sally and the class stopped and stared.

Mama was right, Willow thought. Uncle Ash was an amazing dancer!

The wedding day finally arrived.

"I've never been to a wedding like this before," Cousin Joe whispered to Sadie.

"Isn't it splendid?" Willow said, giving them her most magical smile.

"I'm COLD!"

Willow got Aunt Carol a warm beach blanket to put over her shoulders.

"I have sand in my shoes!"

"You don't need shoes, Aunt Thelma!" Willow said as she wiggled her toes in the soft, warm sand.

"It's hot out here!"

Willow filled a tall glass of lemonade for Uncle Larry. "This will cool you off!"

When the bongo music started, Willow made her way down the aisle.

Uncle Ash was beaming.

At the end of the ceremony, the guests made their way to the reception. Dinner was delicious. Dessert was even better.

When the DJ announced it was time for a special dance, Willow skipped to the dance floor. And when the music started, Willow reached out her hand and said, "Uncle David, it's time to dance!"

No one was surprised to see Uncle Ash standing on the sidelines. Everyone knew Uncle Ash didn't dance.

So when he walked onto the dance floor, everyone was surprised. "What is he doing?" they whispered.

Uncle Ash winked at Willow. Then he took David's hand and began to dance.

Family and friends were astonished at what they saw. Uncle Ash was a magnificent dancer!

Willow twirled Uncle Larry onto the dance floor and jitterbugged with Aunt Thelma too, who was dancing in her bare feet.
Sadie did the Twist, and Cousin Joe showed off his disco moves.
Aunt Carol was swept into Willow's conga line, joining the others on the dance floor.

Even Grandpa found his beat! He had moves no one had ever seen.
And a smile that wouldn't go away. It was easy to see where
Willow and Uncle Ash got their love of dancing.

And for the rest of the night, everyone enjoyed family, friends, and dancing . . .

Especially Willow and her two favorite uncles!

For A.J., my favorite dancer.
—Denise

For Donald, my first ballroom dance teacher and friend.
—Cyd

Sleeping Bear Press™

2395 South Huron Parkway, Suite 200
Ann Arbor MI 48104
www.sleepingbearpress.com

Printed and bound in the United States.

10 9 8 7 6 5 4 3 2 1

Library of Congress Cataloging-in-Publication Data

Names: Brennan-Nelson, Denise, author. | Moore, Cyd, illustrator.
Title: Willow and the wedding / written by Denise Brennan-Nelson ; illustrated by Cyd Moore.
Description: Ann Arbor, MI : Sleeping Bear Press, [2017] | Summary: Bullied
as a gay teenager, especially while performing in a high school musical,
Uncle Ash, who is marrying his boyfriend, refuses to dance at his wedding,
but flower girl Willow is determined to change her favorite uncle's mind.
Identifiers: LCCN 2016030979 | ISBN 9781585369669
Subjects: | CYAC: Dance—Fiction. | Uncles—Fiction. | Bullying—Fiction.|
Weddings—Fiction. | Gays—Fiction.
Classification: LCC PZ7.B75165 Wk 2017 | DDC [E]—dc23
LC record available at https://lccn.loc.gov/2016030979